To ....

For being good.

Merry Christmas!

From **Santa**

Santa is coming to Washington

Written by Steve Smallman
Illustrated by Robert Dunn
Additional artwork by Katherine Kirkland

Sourcebooks and the colophon are registered trademarks of Sourcebooks, Inc.
All rights reserved. No part of this book may be reproduced in any form or by
any electronic or mechanical means including information storage and retrieval
systems—except in the case of brief quotations embodied in critical articles or
reviews—without permission in writing from its publisher, Sourcebooks, Inc.

Published by Sourcebooks Jabberwocky,
an imprint of Sourcebooks, Inc.
P.O. Box 4410, Naperville, Illinois 60567-4410
(630) 961-3900
jabberwockykids.com

Date of Production: May 2019
Run Number: 5014816
Printed and bound in China (1010)
10 9 8 7 6 5 4 3 2 1

Santa is coming to Washington

Written by Steve Smallman

Illustrated by Robert Dunn and Katherine Kirkland

sourcebooks jabberwocky

"Well?"

boomed Santa. "Have all the children from
Washington been good this year?"

"Well...uh...mostly," answered the little old elf,
as he bustled across the busy workshop to
Santa's desk.

Santa peered down at the elf from behind
the tall, teetering piles of letters that the
children of Washington had sent him.

"Mostly?" asked Santa,
looking over the top of his glasses.

"Yes...but they've all been
especially good in the last
few days!" said the elf.

"Jolly good!" chuckled Santa.
"Then we'd better get their presents loaded up!"

Even though the sack of presents was

really, really big
really, really small,

and the elves were

they seemed to have no trouble loading it onto Santa's sleigh.
Though how they managed to fit such a big sack onto one little sleigh
even they didn't know. But somehow they did.

"Splendid!" boomed Santa. "We're ready to go!"

"Er...not quite, Santa,"
said the little old elf. "One of
our reindeer is missing!"

"Missing?

Which reindeer is missing?" asked Santa.

"The youngest one, Santa," said the elf. "It's his first flight tonight. I've called him and called him, but…"

Just then, a young reindeer strolled up, munching on a large carrot.

"Where have you been?"

asked Santa.

But the youngest reindeer was crunching so loudly that it was no wonder he hadn't heard the little old elf calling.

"Oh well, never mind," said Santa, giving the reindeer a little wink. He took out his Santa-nav and tapped in the coordinates for Washington.

"This will guide us to Washington in no time."

CRUNCH!
CRUNCH!
CRUNCH!

With a flick of the reins and
a jerk of the harness, off they
went, racing through the sky.

"Ho, ho, ho!"

laughed Santa.

"We'll soon have these presents
delivered to the Evergreen State!"

Santa's sleigh flew through the starry night, heading south across the Arctic Ocean. On they flew in the crisp, wintry air over Edmonton. In the wink of an eye, the sleigh was flying above Kelowna and on to the Wenatchee National Forest. The youngest reindeer was very excited. He had never been away from the North Pole before.

They had just crossed over Lake Washington
when, suddenly, they ran into a blizzard.
Snowflakes whirled around the sleigh.

They couldn't see a thing!

The youngest reindeer was getting a bit worried,
but Santa didn't seem concerned.

"In two miles..."

said the Santa-nav in a bossy lady's voice,

"...keep left at the next star."

"But, ma'am," Santa blustered, "I can't see any stars in all this snow!"
Soon they were

hopelessly lost!

Ding-dong!
Ding-dong!

Then, through the howling blizzard, the youngest reindeer heard a faint, ringing sound.

Ding-dong!

He looked over at the old reindeer with the red nose. But he had his head down.

(Red nose...I wonder who that could be?)

Ding-dong!
Ding-dong!

Ding-dong! Ding-dong!

There was that sound again, like church bells ringing. The youngest reindeer turned around to look at Santa. But Santa wasn't listening. He seemed to be arguing with a little box with buttons on it.

With a flick of the harness and a jerk of the reins, the youngest reindeer gave a sharp **TUG** and headed off toward the sound of the bells, pulling Santa and his sleigh behind him!

"Whoa!"

cried Santa, pulling his hat straight. "What's going on?" Then, to his surprise, he heard the ringing sound.

"Well done, young reindeer!" he shouted cheerfully. "It must be the bells of St. James Cathedral in Seattle. Don't worry, children, Santa is coming!"

Then, suddenly...

CRUNCH!

The sleigh hit something as it plummeted through the snow clouds. **"You have arrived!"** said the Santa-nav unhelpfully.

The reindeer pulled with all their might until, at last, with a screeching noise, the sleigh scraped clear of the needle and Santa steered them safely over the Pacific Science Center, above Broad Street, along Queen Anne, and down into David Rodgers Park.

Luckily, there
was no real
damage done, but
the packages had all
been jumbled up. Santa
quickly sorted out the
presents into order again.

"All right," said Santa. "Thanks
to this young reindeer I know where
we are now. Don't worry, children,

Santa is coming!"

Santa drove his sleigh expertly from rooftop to rooftop all over Washington, popping in and out of chimneys as fast as he could go.

(Which was pretty fast for a chubby fellow!)

There were big chimneys in Bellevue, and small chimneys in Spokane. He squeezed down thin chimneys in Tacoma and plummeted down fat chimneys in Vancouver.

The youngest reindeer was
amazed at how quickly they went.
Santa never seemed to get tired at all!
And it looked like the children in
Washington were going to be very lucky
this year! But the youngest reindeer
was starting to feel a bit weary
and quite hungry, too!

He piled them under the Christmas trees
and carefully filled up the stockings
with surprises.

In house after house, Santa delved
inside his sack for packages of
every shape and size.

Santa took a little bite out of each cookie,
a tiny sip of milk, wiped his beard,
and popped the carrots into his sack.

In house after house, the good children
of Washington had left out a large plate
of cookies, a small glass of milk,
and a big, crunchy carrot.

From Clallam to Columbia, from Walla Walla to Yakima, from Bainbridge Island to Klickitat, and ALL the places in between, Santa and his sleigh visited every house in Washington.

Santa delivered presents to Andrew, Alison, Anna, Arabella, Archie, Ashley...the list went on and on!...Zac, Zara, Zeb, Zoe, Zybil.

(Zybil? That must be a spelling mistake, surely!)

Finally, Santa had delivered the last present on his long Washington list.

"Great moons and stars!" sighed Santa. "It's past midnight and my sack seems as heavy as ever! I hope I haven't forgotten anyone."

Santa opened his sack to check...but it was full of juicy, crunchy carrots!

Santa divided the carrots among all the reindeer.
"Well done!" he said, patting the youngest reindeer gently on the nose.

But the youngest reindeer didn't hear him...he was too busy munching!

Then it was time to set off for home. Santa reset his Santa-nav for the North Pole,
and soon they were speeding over Mount Rainier, past Port Townsend,
and over Friday Harbor through the crisp, starry night.

"Ho, ho, ho!"
laughed Santa.

"Merry Christmas, Washington!"